PANDA POWER

Welcome to the world of MASK –
MOBILE ARMOURED STRIKE
KOMMAND

Imagine a world where there is more
to reality than meets the eye. Where
illusion and deception team up with
man and machine to create a world of
sophisticated vehicles and weaponry,
manned by agents and counter-agents.

Panda Power

The MASK mission: to discover where
the protected pandas of China have all
been taken and save them from the
machinations of their evil kidnappers –
with the assistance of Matt Trakker,
his son Scott and his faithful
companion T-Bob.

The fifth amazing MASK adventure.

MATT TRAKKER – SPECTRUM

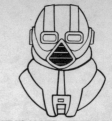

MATT TRAKKER – ULTRA FLASH

BRAD TURNER – HOCUS POCUS

HONDO MACLEAN – BLASTER

BUDDIE HAWKES – PENETRATOR

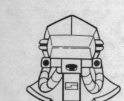

DUSTY HAYES – BACKLASH

BRUCE SATO – LIFTER

ALEX SECTOR – JACKRABBIT

CLIFF DAGGER – THE TORCH

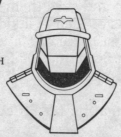

SLY RAX – STILETTO

MILES MAYHEM – VIPER

MASK

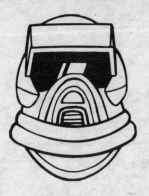

PANDA POWER

novelisation by
Kenneth Harper

Illustrated by Bruce Hogarth

KNIGHT BOOKS
Hodder and Stoughton

With special thanks to Bruce Hogarth and David Lewis
Management for their great help and hard work.

Mask TM and the associated trade marks are the property of
Kenner Parker Toys Inc. (KPT) 1987
Text copyright © Kenneth Harper 1987
Illustrations copyright © Bruce Hogarth 1987

First published by Knight Books 1987

British Library C.I.P.

Harper, Kenneth
    Panda power.—(MASK; 5)
    I. Title   II. Hogarth, Bruce   III. Series
    823'.914[J]   PZ7

    ISBN 0-340-40327-6

Printed and bound in Great Britain for
Hodder and Stoughton Paperbacks, a
division of Hodder and Stoughton Ltd.,
Mill Road, Dunton Green, Sevenoaks,
Kent (Editorial Office: 47 Bedford
Square, London WC1B 3DP) by
Cox & Wyman Ltd., Reading, Berks.
Photoset by Rowland Phototypesetting Ltd.,
Bury St Edmunds, Suffolk.

MASK

ONE

It was late afternoon in the Szechuan province of China. The sun was already low on the distant horizon. Long shadows were cast in the bamboo forest and the shoots took on a dull yellow colour.

Something was moving about in the vegetation. Large, black and white, furry bodies were romping happily. The forest was their home and their playground.

They were extremely rare creatures.

Giant pandas!

Matt Trakker watched them with amused interest. Some of the pandas chased each other, others just strolled along, a few were eating. It was a scene of great contentment. The animals looked warm and

cuddly and at peace. Matt admired them.

He turned to look at a giant among giant pandas.

It was about a hundred foot tall and had enormous hands and legs. The massive face was kind and friendly. For all its bulk, the creature was in no way threatening.

It was a statue, carved out of stone.

Scaffolding covered the giant panda to enable its sculptor to get to any part of the beast. At the moment, he was standing on a platform near the face. Matt was beside him, high above the ground.

The sculptor's name was André. He was a big, handsome man with dark hair and a full beard. His work clearly absorbed him and he was putting the finishing touches to his statue. Using a laser chiselling tool, André shaped the panda's nose a little more. He was a famous and meticulous artist who took great pains with his work. Only when he was satisfied that he had done it correctly did he switch off the laser and stand back with a smile.

'There you are, Matt,' he said, proudly.

'It's magnificent!'

'A teddy bear for all times.'

'If you painted it black and white, André, it could fool a real panda bear. It's one of your finest sculptures.'

'Thanks to you.'

'All I did was watch you,' said Matt with a grin.

'You were the person who brought me here from New York.'

'That's true. But only because I knew you could do it.'

'You're too kind,' replied André, modestly. 'It's an honour to be here in China, making a replica of their National Treasure.'

'It's more than just a statue,' argued Matt.

'I know.'

'It's a symbol of peace.'

'I hope so.'

'The world will meet Panda at its dedication in Peking tomorrow. It will be an important moment, André.'

'I can't wait.'

'An American sculpture in the heart of China. East and West, working together for once. You've done everyone a great service.'

'It was *your* idea, Matt,' reminded the other.

Matt Trakker smiled. He was always looking for ways to improve international relations. The Chinese knew him as a wealthy millionaire with a special interest in paintings and sculptures. What they did not realise was that he was also the head of MASK, the élite team of men whose mission was to combat evil in all its forms.

While Matt and André chatted together up on the scaffolding, two smaller figures came up to the foot of the statue. They looked up.

Scott Trakker was a tousle-haired boy with a mischievous grin. His companion was Thingamebob, the rather funny-looking robot who was called T-Bob for

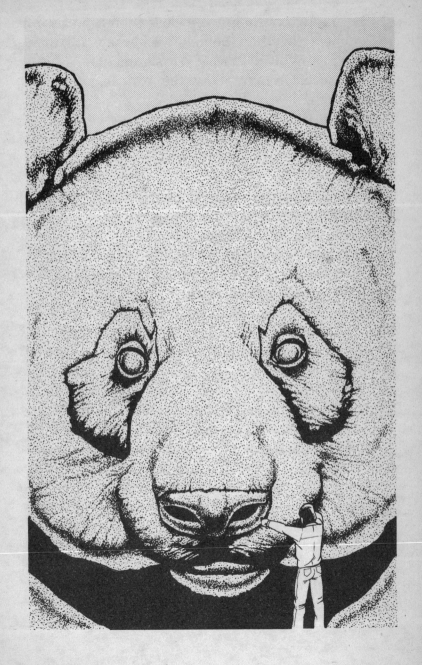

short. The two of them were close friends and went everywhere together. Somehow they always managed to get involved in MASK assignments.

'Dad sure is crazy about the pandas,' observed Scott.

'Yes,' agreed T-Bob in his high, piping voice.

'Guess that's why he helped develop this Preserve.'

'Preserve? I don't see any glass jars.'

'Jars?'

'To keep the fruit in,' explained T-Bob. 'I thought that only strawberries were preserved.'

'This is a *Nature* Preserve.'

'Strawberries come from nature.'

'Don't be silly,' rejoined Scott. 'Pandas have nothing to do with strawberries.'

'Then *they're* the silly ones. Strawberries are delicious.'

'Pandas live on a simple diet, T-Bob. They need a lot of help to survive.'

'Why?'

'Because they're very delicate and rare animals.' He pointed at the robot. 'Sorta like you – only with fur.'

'*Me* like a panda? But we couldn't be *fur*-ther apart!'

Scott groaned at the pun and rolled his eyes.

'That's the worst joke I've heard all day,' he complained.

'Stay around. I can do much worse than that.'

They turned away from the scaffolding and strolled towards the bamboo forest. Two large black and white pandas walked past with a baby panda scampering along behind them. When the baby saw Scott and T-Bob, it ran over to them and sat up on its hind legs.

The robot did not recognise the animal.

'Hey, who let the pooch in here?'

'That's not a pooch, T-Bob. It's a baby bear.'

'Is it?'

They began to pet the creature's head. It started to coo quietly and obviously liked the two friends.

Scott turned to the robot to tease him.

'I'm surprised at you, T-Bob,' he said. 'Don't you know the difference between a dog and a bear?'

'Well, you only taught me the bare necessities.'

Scott groaned at yet another dreadful pun.

'Pandas are vegetarians,' he continued. 'Their favourite food is bamboo shoots. Dogs eat meat.'

'I know what *their* favourite food is.'

'What?'

'Slippers!'

The boy laughed. He gave the baby panda a final pat then it bounded off after its parents. Scott was glad that Matt had given a lot of money to help to set up the Preserve. The pandas were quite delightful animals and needed all the protection they could get.

In the new Preserve, they were completely safe.

Or so it seemed.

Night fell on the bamboo forest. The sky was black and all was silent but for the occasional bleating and cooing of the pandas. A few huts stood on the edge of the

Preserve. They were being used as bedrooms by the visitors from America.

Scott and T-Bob shared a large bed in one hut.

'Listen to the pandas,' said the boy.

'I haven't got any choice.'

'Isn't it a lovely sound?'

The robot tried to imitate the noise without success.

'Coo! Coo!'

'It's great to hear nature,' added Scott.

'Yeah, it sure beats your snoring!'

'I don't snore!'

'Then somebody was in here sawing logs last night.'

'I do *not* snore!' insisted the boy.

'Of course you don't,' teased T-Bob. 'You get up in the dark to open the door so that a herd of wild buffalo can stampede through. And it's *snore* very funny, I can tell you.'

'Your jokes are terrible, T-Bob.'

'It's because I don't get enough sleep.'

Suddenly, a wind blew in through the open window and made the curtains flap. It got wilder and wilder until it was a whooshing, sweeping blast that filled the whole room. The curtains flapped madly and a vase was blown off a dresser. As the wind reached its peak, it even dislodged a painting from the wall and sent it to the ground with a crash.

T-Bob was terrified. He took refuge under the sheets.

'Heeeeeelp!'

'What's going on?' asked Scott.

14

'It sure ain't your snoring this time!'

'Where did that wind come from?'

'Who cares? Just tell it to go away.'

As if hearing him, the fierce wind died away at once. Scott and T-Bob sat up in bed in some alarm. Dead silence reigned over the entire forest.

'Listen!' hissed the boy.

'I can't hear a thing.'

'That's the point, T-Bob.'

'What is?'

'The panda noises have stopped.'

'So?'

'Something's happened. Come on.'

They got out of bed and went to investigate.

Matt Trakker had been disturbed by the commotion as well. A sixth sense warned him that there was trouble about. He came out of his hut and shone the beam of a large flashlight on to the forest. André, the sculptor, was with him. Both men were confused.

'That wind was kinda weird, Matt,' noted André.

'Very weird. Came and went so quickly.'

'And it's such a mild night.'

Scott and T-Bob came out of their hut.

'What's going on, Dad?' called the boy.

'I'm not sure,' admitted Matt, 'but I've never seen Mother Nature hit 'n' run like that before.'

His torch searched the bamboo forest. There was no sign of the animals. The stillness was quite eerie.

'It's so quiet,' said André. 'Where are the bears?'

'I can barely see,' piped T-Bob.

The beam of the flashlight detected a movement among the vegetation. It was the baby panda who had befriended Scott and T-Bob earlier on. The creature was bleating pitifully for its mother and father. When it saw Scott, it ran over to him and sprang up into his arms. The boy was taken aback.

'He sure is scared!'

'What are we supposed to do with him?' asked T-Bob.

'He needs some comfort, that's all,' said Scott.

'You two can take care of him for now,' decided Matt.

'Wonder what happened to his mom and dad,' said André.

Matt Trakker feared the worst.

'They've disappeared. My guess is that all the pandas have gone. This little fella is the only survivor. Someone must have rustled the others.'

But *how*?

Where could all the pandas be?

It was a question that only MASK would be able to answer.

TWO

As soon as the sun was up next morning, Matt Trakker led the way to Thunder Hawk, his specially designed MASK vehicle. Scott and T-Bob were delighted when he allowed them to go on the trip. They sat in the rear seat with their safety belts clipped into position. Matt pressed a button and the sports car converted to jet mode.

Thunder Hawk was soon spearing up into the sky.

'Keep your eyes peeled,' said Matt.

'Can't see a thing, Dad,' answered Scott.

'Nor me,' added T-Bob.

'But there were *hundreds* of pandas down there yesterday,' insisted Matt. 'Let's take a closer look.'

He brought Thunder Hawk down so that it skimmed across the top of the bamboo forest. Though they covered the whole Preserve a couple of times, they saw no pandas at all. The only one left seemed to be the baby panda who was now sitting on Scott's knee and nibbling contentedly at some parsnips.

The boy looked out through the window and saw some deep marks in the forest, almost as if something had been dragged along.

'What are those funny scrape marks down there, Dad?'

'I don't know,' replied Matt. 'But there doesn't seem to be a single panda left on the Preserve.'

'No single ones,' joked T-Bob. 'Any married ones?'

'This is no time for wisecracks,' sighed Scott.

'Sorry.'

'I don't get it,' continued the boy. 'How could all those bears disappear like that?'

The robot could not resist another awful pun.

'Must be a bad case of panda-monium!'

'T-Bob!' protested Scott.

'Whatever it was,' decided Matt Trakker, 'I'm going to get the bare facts!'

'Don't *you* start as well, Dad!'

They all laughed. Even the baby panda joined in.

Matt abandoned the search and brought the aircraft down in the clearing by the huts. His worst fears had been confirmed. The pandas had been taken away in the night.

It had indeed been an ill wind.

André supervised the loading of his statue on to the flat-bed trailer of a huge semi-truck. Chains were used to hold the sculpture in place. André had spent a long time on his work of art and he did not want it damaged in transit. When the loading was completed, he walked around the trailer to make a final check.

Matt Trakker came over to join him.

'That's *one* panda they didn't steal, André.'

'Far too heavy.'

'And too big. They'd have a job hiding it.'

'It beats me,' confided the sculptor. 'How can anyone be so cruel as to steal innocent animals?'

'I wish I knew that, André.'

'Well, when you find out, just let *me* have a go at the people responsible. There are a few things I'd like to say to them.'

'I'm sure. Everything ready?'

'Just about. I'm riding shotgun.'

'Don't blame you.'

'I want to make certain my statue gets there in one piece.'

'See you at Tien An Men Square for the celebration.'

'I'll be there, Matt.'

'So will this guy.'

Matt gave the sculpture a playful pat.

André got into the passenger seat of the cab and the truck started up. It moved slowly away with its precious cargo. The statue would be the centrepiece in the dedication ceremony that was going to be held in Peking.

André's work would be honoured in the Chinese capital.

Matt was about to walk away when another vehicle arrived. It was a big, black sedan car and it stopped nearby. The rear door opened and a man stepped out. He was in his forties, had a distinguished look about him and wore a plain suit with patch pockets and a cap of the same colour. He bowed politely to Matt.

'Mr Trakker?' questioned the newcomer, offering his hand.

'Yes.'

'I'm Chin Ho, The National Wildlife Representative.'

Matt shook hands with him and smiled.

'Nice to meet you, Chin Ho.'

'We got your message.'

'Then you know about the missing pandas.'

'Unhappily, yes,' said the Chinaman. 'It is very worrying. Especially as there has been other bad news.'

'Oh?'

'It is not only the Preserve that has lost its pandas.'

'What do you mean?'

'My rangers report other panda kidnappings.'

'Where?'

'In every region where the creature lives.'

'All over China?'

'Yes,' admitted Chin Ho. 'My rangers have searched by air and land. Only a few bears appear to remain in the whole country.'

'Wow!'

'You can understand why we are so concerned.'

'I can,' agreed Matt. 'Listen, Chin Ho. I'd like to try to find out why your pandas are suddenly going from a "vanishing breed" to a vanished one! If we don't do something quickly, the panda could become extinct.'

'I wish you good fortune, Mr Trakker.'

'Thank you.'

'But I will not be able to keep this from the Chinese people for long. It is a national tragedy.'

'I appreciate that.'

'When will you start?'

'As soon as the dedication of the statue is over.'

'China will be eternally grateful to you.'

'I just hope I can find those pandas for you.'

'They are wonderful creatures.'

'Yeah. Real cute.'

The men shook hands again then Chin Ho left in his car.

Matt considered the latest crisis that faced him.

A monstrous crime had been committed.

He had a sneaking idea that he knew who was behind it all.

VENOM.

Easter Island was a small, triangular piece of land with long-dead volcanoes at each apex. Its landscape was marked with megalithic stone faces which reflected a prehistoric culture. The carvings varied in height from three to thirty or more feet.

23

For many years, Easter Island had been uninhabited but it had a lot of visitors now. Hundreds of giant pandas were meandering about. They had been brought from all over China to form a colony. Food was plentiful and they grazed among the statues.

Miles Mayhem stood on a hill and gazed down on the stone figures below. The VENOM leader was wearing his usual military uniform and stroking his moustache with an air of self-importance. Beside him was Cliff Dagger, an ugly brute of a man who was one of his main agents.

Mayhem's voice was more boastful than ever.

'At last, VENOM will be immortalised!'

'What's "immortalised" mean?' wondered Dagger.

'It means that you're an idiot!'

'Does it?'

'*Everybody* knows what the word means!'

'I don't.'

'That's why you're an idiot!'

'So tell me, Mayhem. What happens if we get immortalised?'

'It means we'll be in the history books forever.'

'We'll be *famous*?'

'More than that, Dagger. We'll be infamous!'

'Ah.'

Mayhem surveyed the island like a mighty conqueror looking over a great empire. He struck a pose.

'I've dreamed of this for years.'

Dagger shrugged. 'Well, being stuck out here on

Easter Island with all these bears is a sort of nightmare, if you ask me.'

'I *didn't* ask you, imbecile!'

Before Mayhem could yell any more at his henchman, he was diverted by the noise of an aircraft approaching fast. Manta swooped down out of the sky. It was in jet mode and was being piloted by another VENOM agent, Vanessa Warfield.

A new feature had been added to the aircraft. Attached to the front was a large, steel scoop the door of which was closed tight. Manta came in to land and ended up at the base of the hill where the two men were standing.

Vanessa Warfield emerged from the aircraft with her colleague, Sly Rax. She was a sharp-featured young woman with a black streak in her hair and he was a villainous-looking thug with a moustache and a tufted beard. Vanessa reached inside Manta to switch on a control lever. The door on the scoop opened immediately.

Several pandas peered out nervously and then wandered out on to the grass. When they saw the other animals grazing nearby, they went off to join them.

Vanessa called up to Miles Mayhem.

'That's the last of 'em. And the ship has been unloaded, too.'

'Good.'

A few of the bears moved towards Rax who did not like them.

'Get away!' he growled.

26

Dagger laughed. 'Guess they don't go for your after-shave lotion, Rax!'

'Get outta here!' warned Rax. 'Or I'll make bearskin rugs outta ya!'

The bears scurried away in fear.

'Where's the sculptor?' demanded Mayhem.

'We couldn't get him in the open to scoop him up,' said Vanessa Warfield. 'We had to give up.'

'Give up!' roared Mayhem. 'Give UP!!!!'

'Only for the time being,' argued Vanessa, backing away.

The VENOM leader came down the hill to confront them.

Dagger was glad that *he* was not facing Mayhem's wrath.

'Whaddaya think that sculptor is gonna do?' shouted the evil genius. 'Give you a written invitation to kidnap him!'

'No,' confessed Rax.

'No,' added Vanessa.

'Now, go get him!' ordered Mayhem. 'And don't come back without him. He is vital to the VENOM cause.'

Vanessa and Rax went back to Manta and climbed in. Within seconds, they took off in a cloud of dust, leaving Mayhem and Dagger coughing in their wake.

The capture of André was essential to their plan.

VENOM wanted more than power this time.

They wanted glory as well.

THREE

T-Bob sat on a chair in the hut that he shared with Scott Trakker. The compartment at the front of the robot's chest was open and a whole mass of complex wiring and circuitry was exposed. Scott was unplugging some wires before connecting them up to different sockets. Eventually, after a lot of experimenting, the boy found two wires that produced an electric spark when they touched.

T-Bob shivered slightly and giggled.

'Hey, that tickles!'

'Maybe I'm working close to your funny bone,' said Scott.

'All my bones are funny!'

Scott laughed and continued to work away inside

29

the open compartment. Watching them from the bed was the baby panda who was cooing softly. He seemed to understand that it was all for his benefit.

A box-like pouch had been fixed to T-Bob's chest. It was similar to a marsupial's pouch except that it was lined with soft cloth and wired up at the back.

'Is all this really necessary?' asked T-Bob.

'He's going to need body warmth,' explained Scott, nodding towards the baby panda. 'We've got to get him to his mother and father as soon as possible.'

'I go along with that.'

'Meanwhile . . .'

'Here comes the catch!'

'*You've* gotta be his mom!'

'Why me?'

'Because you've got the right equipment, T-Bob.'

'But I don't *want* to be a mom!'

'Hold still. I've almost finished.'

Scott made some more adjustments inside the compartment.

'I'm starting to feel warm,' said T-Bob.

'That's because I'm "hot wiring" you.'

'You're *what*!'

'I'm helping to turn you into the world's only walk-ing, talking incubator.'

T-Bob looked down at the pouch on his chest and sighed.

'I'm not sure this is such a good idea,' he argued. 'I mean, I'm gonna look like a kangaroo.'

'You mean a kangaroobot!'

It was T-Bob's turn to groan at an appalling joke.

Another spark was set off inside the robot's chest and he went off into a peel of laughter. Scott made a final adjustment then closed the compartment and stood back. Now only the box-pouch was in view on T-Bob's chest.

'Okay,' said the boy. 'The thermostat will regulate the exact temperature of a mother panda.'

'That's all I need!'

Scott picked up the baby bear and lowered it gently into the box. It snuggled into the warmth and obviously felt secure. It began to coo more loudly to show its appreciation.

'T-Bob, you make the perfect mother.'

'You would have to say that!'

Scott took a baby's bottle from a paper bag nearby and handed it over to the robot. The bottle was still warm.

'And this will make you even better.'

'I'd rather be a dad – not a mom!'

'Give your baby the bottle.'

'It's not *my* baby,' protested T-Bob.

'Coo! Coo!'

The panda rolled its eyes affectionately and gave the robot a smile. T-Bob patted the animal on the head and gave it the bottle. Putting the teet to its mouth, the bear started to drink the milk.

'Well, we oughta get going,' decided Scott. 'We're supposed to meet Dad at Tien An Men Square for the statue dedication.'

'What about the panda?'

'He comes with us, T-Bob. Where *you* go, baby goes.'

The three of them left the hut together.

Tien An Men Square was a vast open space at the heart of Peking. It was surrounded by civic buildings in the Chinese capital and most of them were pagoda-style. The panda statue that had been commissioned by Matt Trakker stood in the middle of the square. It was held up by scaffolding and there was a portable elevator which could rise up to the face of the sculpture.

A small group of people stood at the base of the statue. They included Matt, André, Chin Ho and various Chinese dignitaries.

'It's a fine piece of work,' congratulated Chin Ho.

'Thanks,' said André.

'Very lifelike,' added Matt.

'I'd just like to check the facial features once more,' announced the sculptor. 'I'm starting to like pandas as much as you.'

'You're such a perfectionist, André.'

'Have we got time, Matt?'

'Yes. I'll come up with you.'

Chin Ho lifted a wrist to check his watch.

'The crowds will not arrive for two hours.'

Matt led the way across to the elevator. He and André were soon making the journey skyward to the top of the statue. Chin Ho and his colleagues looked on with admiration.

Scott and T-Bob were nearby. Several market stalls had been set up in the square and the friends were standing beside the cart of a greengrocer. The baby panda was finishing off a bottle of milk. When it was empty, the bear held it out and bleated plaintively.

'Wow!' exclaimed T-Bob. 'He's hungry again.'

'How much has he had so far?'

'That's the second bottle since we got here.'

'We're gonna have to get him his own cow,' noted Scott.

T-Bob began to rattle noisily in alarm.

'I am *not* carrying a cow around in my pouch!' Another thought struck him. 'Hey, what happens if we can't find the real mom and dad?'

'You keep on minding baby.'

'But baby will grow to be much bigger than me!'

'Fine,' agreed Scott. 'So we have this pouch made for the bear and *he* can carry *you*.'

T-Bob gave a sigh of resignation and found another bottle of milk for the animal. It cooed its thanks and drank on.

Matt and André, meanwhile, had reached the top of the statue. The sculptor was casting a critical eye over his handiwork. He smoothed over the great stone face with the palm of his hand. André wanted everything to be perfect for the dedication ceremony.

'That's all they've got left,' observed Matt.

'Yes,' sighed André. 'A *stone* panda. I sure would like to see the real ones back again. I hate to lose my models.'

'We'll find 'em!' promised Matt.

'How?'

'Leave that to me.'

André suddenly shivered. It was a bright, sunny day and he could not understand why he felt cold. Then Matt shivered.

'What's going on?' asked the sculptor.

'Feels like that wind again.'

'The one we had last night?'

Matt's guess was correct. The first whispers soon became a violent gust as the wind swept across the square. It made the market stalls flap and people cowered from the blast. Up on the statue, the two friends clung on to the scaffolding for safety as the wind whipped around them.

They soon saw the cause of it all high above them.

It was Manta in whisper mode.

VENOM was at work once more.

Generating the vicious wind, the aircraft dived down at full speed and aimed for the statue. Vanessa Warfield was at the controls and Sly Rax was alongside her.

'There he is!' she said, spotting André.

'This'll give 'em a shock!' added Rax.

'Yeah – wait till the newspapers get this *scoop*!'

She hit a switch and the door on the scoop opened.

The wind was now blowing at such gale force that Matt and André were holding on to the scaffolding for dear life. Then the sculptor lost his grip on the poles and teetered on the planking.

Manta descended on him in a flash.

'André – look out!' warned Matt.

'Aaaaaah!!!!'

Matt reached out to save him but he was too late.

Operating the controls, Vanessa made the scoop dip down and shovel up the sculptor. André was kidnapped with remarkable ease. The door of the scoop clanged shut on him and he was trapped in the dark.

The VENOM agents were pleased with their work.

'Got him!' asserted Vanessa.

'In the bag!' said Rax.

'This should keep Mayhem quiet.'

'Yeah. We caught his sculpture alive and well.'

'*Sculptor*,' corrected Vanessa.

'Uh?'

'Sculptor not sculpture. A sculptor is the person who makes a sculpture. If we'd caught the sculpture, we'd have that statue of the panda in our scoop.'

'It would never go in!' said Rax with a laugh.

He looked over his shoulder at the massive structure behind him and his laugh turned to a cheer. When Manta had grabbed André from the scaffolding, the scoop had knocked against the planking and cracked it badly. The crack had now got very much worse.

'Hey!' shouted Rax. 'Mayhem's gonna love us!'

'That'll be a change!'

'Looks like we killed two birds with one stone.'

'What are you on about, Rax?'

'Matt Trakker. Take a peep.'

'I will.'

Vanessa swung Manta round in a curve so that she could look back down at the square. She, too, was delighted by what she saw. It was an incidental bonus to their crime.

Matt Trakker was staring death in the face.

The wooden platform on which he was standing was now split right down the middle. He tried to grab the rope that hung from the statue but it was beyond his reach. The whole platform splintered without warning and he was thrown helplessly into the air.

There was fear and horror down in the square when people saw what was happening. A man was hurtling down towards them. If he hit the brick foundation of the square, then he would be smashed to a pulp. Cries of apprehension went up on all sides.

Matt Trakker seemed almost certain to perish.

The future of MASK hung in the balance.

FOUR

Unable to save himself, Matt Trakker fell through space. The ground seemed to be racing up to hit him and he feared the worst. Chin Ho and the dignitaries were transfixed. They were convinced that they were about to witness a hideous accident in Tien An Men Square.

Fortunately, somebody was on hand to come to the rescue.

Scott, T-Bob and the baby panda stared upward.

Then the boy sprung into action.

'Come on, T-Bob! Gimme a hand!'

'With what?'

'This cart! *Quick!*'

The two of them grabbed hold of the greengrocer's

cart and rapidly wheeled it into position. They were just in time. Instead of hitting the hard ground, Matt made a soft landing in a huge pile of ripe tomatoes.

SQUELCH!!!!

'Ohhhhh!' yelled T-Bob.

'Ughhhh!' added Scott.

'Coo!' said the panda.

They had saved Matt's life but they were now covered in red juice as a result. The impact had been so great that the juice went all over them. It was a small price to pay for the safety of the leader of MASK.

When Matt climbed out of the cart, he was plastered from head to foot in squashed tomatoes. Even Chin Ho laughed. The greengrocer was less amused. His day's produce had been ruined.

Matt scraped off the worst of the mess.

'Thanks, Scott,' he said with feeling. 'You, too, T-Bob.'

'Coo!'

'Don't forget baby, Dad. *He* helped.'

'Yes,' moaned T-Bob. 'I have to cart him every-where.'

Matt looked down at the state he was in and chuckled.

'Any crackers to go with this tomato soup?'

'Next time, Dad,' said Scott.

'I'd better get cleaned up,' decided Matt.

'It was VENOM, wasn't it?' asked the boy.

'Yes, Scott.'

His expression became serious as he gazed up at the sky. Manta was no more than a spot in the heavens now. Matt shook his head in bewilderment.

'It's obvious they stole the bears as well,' he concluded. 'But *why*? And what could they possibly want with André?'

T-Bob looked at the squashed tomatoes and thought of a joke.

'We'll have to *ketchup* with them and ask!'

They all groaned in mock pain. The baby panda yawned.

Manta landed on Easter Island and Mayhem stepped forward to greet it. The door on the scoop opened and a confused André stumbled out. He found himself face to face with the leader of VENOM.

'Welcome to Easter Island!' said Mayhem.

André looked around and saw all the pandas.

'*You* stole them from the Preserve.'

'It suited my purposes,' said the other, airily.

'Why am I here?' demanded the sculptor.

'To complete the most important commission of your career.'

'But I've done that. It was the giant panda.'

Miles Mayhem drew himself up to his full height.

'You are going to carve a statue of *me*.'

'Yeah,' said Rax, who had got out of Manta. 'Mayhem wanted the best man for the job and he heard how good you were at making statues of animals.' He saw the fury in his leader's eyes and backed away at once. 'Hey, don't get me wrong. I didn't mean that *you* were an animal. In fact –'

'Rax!!!!' roared Mayhem.

'What?'

'SHUT UP!!!!'

André was torn between fear and amusement.

'Why do you want a statue of yourself?' he wondered. 'To frighten the birds away like a scarecrow?'

'Don't mock me!' warned Mayhem. 'Just do as you're told.'

'Supposing I won't play ball?' asked André.

'You will,' insisted the other.

'And supposing I won't?'

'Then I'll have to apply some artistic inspiration,' he announced. 'With this.'

He pulled a gun from his pocket and aimed it at André. The sculptor quailed and realised that he had no choice. VENOM had the advantage over him. He gulped and nodded in agreement.

'Okay, I'll do it.'

Mayhem cackled. 'I had a feeling you might. It's a privilege for you to be asked. Not every sculptor gets the chance to immortalise VENOM. You're going to carve the statue of a future leader of the world.'

'Who's that?' said Rax with interest.

'ME!!!!' howled his master.

'Oh, yeah. Of course.'

'Right!' commanded Mayhem. 'Let's get started!'

He took André across to a massive hunk of stone.

Against his will, the sculptor got to work.

Matt Trakker wasted no time in assembling the MASK agents who could help him in this particular assignment. Sitting inside Thunder Hawk, he was able to flick a switch and patch into the computer back at his headquarters by means of a satellite. He gave his orders into a microphone.

'Scan the personnel files for the agents best suited for this assignment.'

The computer screen in front of him bleeped and whirred, then punched up a graphic rendition of the face of each agent as he was named. A picture of the respective vehicle was also displayed.

The computer's voice was flat, female and impersonal.

'Personnel selected – Alex Sector, computer and communications expert. Rhino systems commander. Animal expertise critical.'

'Approved,' said Matt.

The computer screen scrambled then rearranged to expose a familiar face. The same vehicle was shown.

'Bruce Sato. Mechanical engineer and design specialist. Vehicle Code Name – Rhino. Lifter mask and design skills essential.'

'Approved.'

'Hondo MacLean. Weapons specialist, tactical strategist. Vehicle Code Name – Firecracker. All terrain vehicles potential necessary.'

'Personnel approved,' announced Matt. 'Assemble Mobile Armoured Strike Kommand!'

As he gave the order, he looked down at his wrist-watch and pressed a tiny button. The liquid-crystal display began to flash.

MASK was on the move once more.

The signal went across the world in an instant. Each of the three agents chosen responded immediately to the call.

Alex Sector, owner of an exotic pet store, was sitting at his desk to catch up on his paperwork. Around his neck was a small scarf. As soon as his wristwatch flashed and buzzed, the scarf came to life. It was in fact a ferret and it jumped down on to the desk in alarm. Alex caught it, put it into a cage with some other ferrets, then went out of the shop at speed.

Bruce Sato, a toy designer, was testing out some boomerangs he had made. He stood in a park and hurled them away one by one but they failed to return. His boomerangs all seemed to be duds. Then he got his summons on the watch and he forgot all about his work. Hurling the other boomerangs away, he went racing off. A few seconds later, all of the boomerangs returned to the point from which they had been thrown.

Hondo MacLean, a High School teacher, was in his office. He hated marking papers yet he had an enormous pile to work through. As he read the first essay and corrected it, he got his call from MASK. Delighted at the excuse to stop, he put his papers aside and ran out.

46

Three brave agents with a single mission.
To find the missing pandas.

André had never had a more unpleasant commission. He was carving the evil features of Miles Mayhem on the stone. Instead of using a new piece, he had decided to change one of the existing stone carvings so that it resembled the VENOM leader. That speeded up his job greatly.

Mayhem was not the most patient of models. He held a rigid pose with his chin jutting out and his thick eyebrows meeting in a ferocious scowl. His voice was a bellow of irritation.

'Hurry up!'

'You cannot rush a sculptor,' argued André.

'I can do *anything*!' insisted the other. 'We brought you those laser chisels so that you could work fast. So get a move on.'

'If I rush, I'll make mistakes.'

'It must be absolutely *perfect*!'

'That's impossible.'

'Why?'

'Haven't you looked at yourself in a mirror recently?'

'Be quiet!' snarled Mayhem.

André shrugged and continued to chip away at the stone with his laser chisel. He was slowly converting the blank face of some prehistoric person into the large, ugly countenance of Miles Mayhem.

'This statue will live forever!' boasted the model.

'Don't be so sure.'

'The day will come when a statue of me will be set up in the Tien An Men Square. The Chinese will flock to see me.'

'So that they can throw rotten eggs at you.'

'So that they can *worship* me!' proclaimed Mayhem. 'This statue is only the first of many. When VENOM is triumphant, a bust of me will stand in every capital in the world.'

André chiselled on in fear.

He was not just dealing with a highly dangerous man.

Mayhem was evidently crazed with power. He was mad.

When his agents arrived at the Preserve to begin the search, Matt Trakker took them off to see the gouged earth. Alex, Bruce and Hondo knelt to examine the deep scrape that had been made.

Matt ran a hand inside the hollow.

'This was caused by the scoop VENOM used to kidnap both the bears and André.'

Bruce nodded. 'Silent thieves in the night.'

'Yes,' agreed his leader. 'Manta must have been using whisper mode when they grabbed the pandas. We didn't hear the sound of her engines – only the wind.'

'Makes sense,' added Alex. 'But what's the connection between the pandas and André? Why take him as well?'

'That's a tough question,' admitted Matt, 'but here's an even tougher one. Where are they now?'

Alex Sector plucked at his full beard.

'Pandas are delicate. They rarely survive outside China because their food source is here.'

'Since most of the pandas have gone,' noted Hondo, 'VENOM must have taken them to a place with a comparable food source.'

'Good thinking!' said Matt. 'That could be the handle we're looking for – their food source!'

'Well, they like a taste or two of wild parsnips,' explained Alex. 'Like that little sonofagun.'

He pointed to the baby panda who was being fed on parsnips by Scott and T-Bob. The bear was munching away happily.

'But what they really *love*,' continued Alex, 'is bamboo. To them, it's a delicacy – Panda candy!'

Matt broke off a bamboo shoot and took it over to the baby panda. He gobbled it at once and smacked his lips with pleasure.

'Coo!'

'You're welcome, partner,' said Matt with a smile.

'Can you believe it, T-Bob?' asked Scott. 'The baby bear is just crazy for bamboo.'

The robot looked up hopefully.

'Does this mean he's going off the bottle?'

'Afraid not,' replied Matt. 'But it does mean we may be able to find his mom and dad.'

'Coo!'

'And "coo" to you, too,' returned T-Bob.

The MASK leader swung round to face his agents.

'China's the only country that can support pandas with bamboo. And since most of them are gone, let's assume the bears must be living on wild parsnips somewhere else.'

'Sounds like a job for our computer,' decided Alex.

'Let's go,' added Bruce.

The four men went back to Rhino and climbed inside. Alex sat in front of the computer console and fed information by tapping it out on the keyboard.

'Panda bear, secondary food source, wild parsnips . . . Now we need a country and a precise location within it.'

The computer began to whirr and its screen flashed up map graphics of various countries. Pictures of panda bears also appeared.

Matt watched it all intently.

'Hope it can come up with the recipe for this one.'

'Well,' said Alex, 'I've given the computer everything it needs except tea and crumpets!'

Suddenly, the flashing stopped and the screen was filled with a map of an island. Information was typed up underneath the map and Matt Trakker leaned forward to read it out.

'Large numbers of pandas can survive on the wild parsnips of Easter Island . . .' His face puckered with curiosity. 'Pandas on Easter Island. That's what I call a mixed bag!'

They had taken a first important step.

VENOM had been found.

It was time for MASK to swing into action.
'Easter Island!' ordered Matt.
His agents were as eager to get there as he was.

FIVE

Thunder Hawk streaked across the blue sky at top speed and left a blaze of white in its wake. Matt Trakker was at the controls and Bruce Sato was beside him, studying the video scanner that was focused on the sea below. Land came into view and Bruce was fascinated by what he saw.

Matt took the aircraft down to a lower altitude.

'How does Easter Island look at five thousand feet?'

'Like a perfect panda cage without bars.'

The prehistoric heads came up on the screen then Bruce spotted some movement among them. He fiddled with the switches until he got a close-up. Surprise made him sit up at once.

'Matt – take a look!'

'What at?'

'It's André. With Mayhem!'

'Where?'

Matt was as amazed as his colleague by what he saw.

Far below them, André was standing on scaffolding that had been set up against one of the carved heads. Using laser sculpting equipment, he was altering the statue into the image of the VENOM leader who had struck an arrogant pose.

Vanessa, Rax and Dagger were guarding the hapless André.

'Hurry it up, Mr Sculptor!' commanded Mayhem. 'Or you're gonna retire here.'

André shivered. 'I don't think I'd like your pension plan.'

Inside Thunder Hawk, the video scanner was showing pictures of the pandas, wandering about the island and feeding off wild parsnips. The animals looked quite untroubled and totally harmless.

'The pandas are safe and sound,' observed Bruce.

'That's more than can be said for poor André!'

'Yes. What a terrible commission for any sculptor!'

'To be forced to carve *that* ugly mug!'

'Miles Mayhem must be drunk with power.'

'I thought VENOM had tried everything,' said Matt with disgust. 'But this time they've gone right over the top!'

He brought Thunder Hawk in for a lower sweep.

Down below on the island, the VENOM agents heard the noise of the aircraft and gazed up. André's hopes stirred at once when he saw that his friend had tracked him down. Vanessa, Rax and Dagger seemed upset but their leader was quite calm.

'I was wondering when MASK would get here!'

'Are you sure your bear farm's gonna work?' asked Vanessa.

'Of course. Don't worry about it.'

'If they attack now,' said Dagger, 'we're sitting ducks!'

'They won't attack,' promised Mayhem.

'Yes, they will,' decided Rax.

He cowered in fear as Thunder Hawk came in low and fast over the heads of the statues. But there was no assault. The aircraft simply flew past then soared back up into the sky.

Mayhem cackled and his colleagues were relieved.

'Just as I predicted!' said the VENOM leader. 'MASK didn't fire one skinny little laser!'

'What happens when they *do* attack?' wondered Dagger.

'They won't attack, airhead! Who'd want to attack a teddy bear?'

Dagger saw the joke and burst into coarse laughter.

'So that's why we brought all those pandas here!' he said. 'They *protect* us!'

'Exactly!'

'You're a genius, Mayhem.'

'Like I always told you – I'm not just a pretty face!'

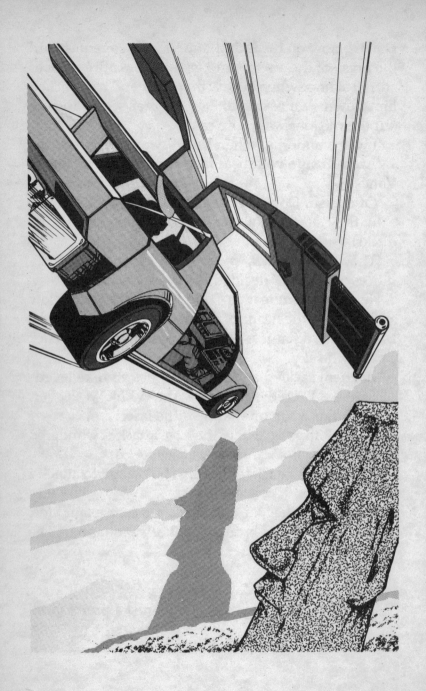

André bit back a comment and began to chisel away again.

VENOM had definitely got the upper hand.

He was trapped.

Matt Trakker was always realistic. He knew that he had been outflanked by his arch-enemy and he was ready to admit it. As he took Thunder Hawk over the horizon, he turned to his co-pilot.

'We're stymied, Bruce.'

'For the moment, maybe.'

'If we try to rescue André and save those famous statues, the panda bears could be hurt bad. Or even killed!'

'Mayhem has thought it out very carefully.'

'You can say that again!'

'One can see in all directions from the island. VENOM's shrine also makes the perfect headquarters. It's a fortress.'

'Yeah,' sighed Matt. 'VENOM Island! And the pandas are his insurance policy against attack.'

'That's a high-priced premium.'

Bruce Sato was known among MASK agents for his wisdom. It was often expressed in a cryptic way but it was no less useful for that. Matt applied to his colleague once more.

'Is there anything in a fortune cookie about this?'

'Look to the creatures, Matt, for *they* have the answer.'

'The creatures?'

'Think about it,' advised the other.

Matt did and an idea soon came. A grin surfaced.

'You're right, Bruce,' he agreed. 'The animals themselves. I've got a marvellous idea for a plan.'

Bruce Sato guessed what it would be.

'We'll call it – Panda Power!'

MASK had found a way to strike back, after all.

The small village was on the far side of Easter Island. It consisted of rough houses arranged in narrow streets. Thunder Hawk was parked on the edge of the village, still in jet mode. Bruce Sato was standing beneath the aircraft so that he could attach claw-like clamps to the underside. Nearby was a large steel ramp that rested on long, metal legs.

Matt Trakker scanned the heavens. The heavy drone of an aeroplane was heard and he was pleased. He checked his watch.

'Right on schedule!'

'All finished here,' said Bruce, stepping back.

They moved across to an open field and watched the transport plane come into land. As soon as it had taxied to a halt, it let down a huge ramp to reveal Rhino and Firecracker. The MASK vehicles drove down the ramp and on to the ground.

Alex Sector got out of Rhino. With him were Scott and T-Bob. The baby panda was in the boy's arms. Hondo joined them from Firecracker.

'Hi, Dad!' called Scott.

'Hi. How was your flight?'

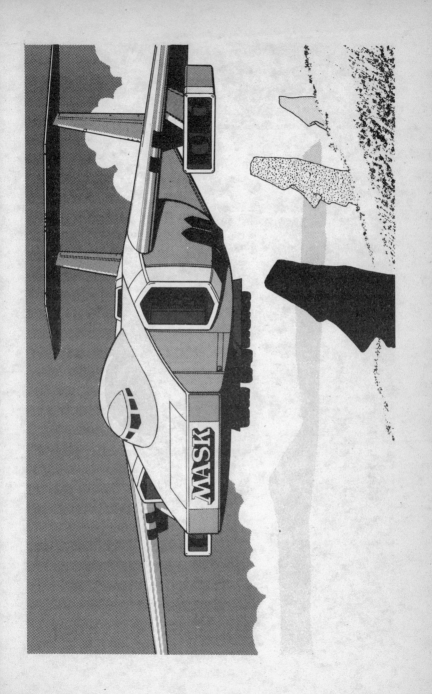

'Bumpy,' complained Alex.

'And no first class accommodation!' moaned Hondo.

The baby panda jumped from Scott's arms and landed on T-Bob's head before climbing down into the incubator. The animal nestled down.

'Baby loved it,' said the boy. 'He slept almost all the way during the flight. Like a real baby.'

'Yes,' sighed T-Bob, looking very weary. 'Now he's gonna be awake all *day*! Oh dear!'

Scott smiled. 'It's all part of being a mother.'

'Cheer up, T-Bob,' urged Matt. 'I wanted you and Scott to come here so we can re-unite him with his mom and dad.' He turned to the agents. 'VENOM is playing at little King of the Castle. We're gonna knock them off their throne.'

'How?' asked Hondo.

'You'll see.'

At that moment, a cargo elevator inside the transport plane lowered a large wooden crate down to the ground. Matt gave a signal and the pilot took the plane back up into the sky.

The MASK leader patted the crate with confidence.

'Gentlemen – this is Panda Power.'

'What's that?' said Alex.

'Our secret weapon. Bruce has designed a carriage rack under Thunder Hawk that will hold it.'

Alex and Hondo applauded playfully. Bruce bowed.

'Once we're set,' continued Matt, 'I want Rhino and

61

Firecracker out of VENOM's sight. I'm going to drop the crate away from the statues. Then the fun begins. Any questions?'

'Just one,' replied Alex. 'When do we leave.'

'Straight away.' He signalled with an arm. 'Bruce!'

Bruce Sato put on his distinctive Lifter mask.

He aimed it at the ramp and gave a command.

'Lifter – on!'

The anti-gravity beam shot out of the mask and lifted the ramp some twenty feet into the air. Bruce guided it across until it was above the wooden crate and then he lowered it down. The ramp now held the crate firmly in place with its steel legs.

Lifter's ray stopped. Bruce now directed his mask at Thunder Hawk and gave the order again. The beam streaked out to hit the MASK vehicle and lifted it up as if it were as light as a feather. Bruce brought Thunder Hawk down on top of the ramp.

Alex and Hondo ran to the wooden crate and climbed its framework till they reached the top. They attached Thunder Hawk's new clamps to the crate then jumped down again. Everything was now ready for take-off.

Scott looked on with fascination. The baby panda was still in his incubator. T-Bob seemed to be exhausted.

'Do we come with you?' asked the robot.

'Sorry, T-Bob,' said Matt. 'Stay here while we try to arrange a family reunion for your little pal.'

Matt tossed a rope ladder out of the side of Thunder

Hawk and Bruce Sato climbed up it and got into the passenger seat. The vehicle took off.

Hondo and Alex ran off to their own transports. Within seconds they had also sped away in a whirl of dust.

MASK was launching its attack on VENOM.

Panda Power was about to take over.

SIX

Thick forest surrounded the clearing where the carved heads were standing. Miles Mayhem was still holding his pose while André put the final touches to the statue. Vanessa Warfield, Sly Rax and Cliff Dagger watched the sculptor at work. Pandas grazed peacefully all around them. It was a tranquil scene.

None of the VENOM team realised that Rhino and Firecracker were hidden nearby in the forest. Having approached stealthily, the MASK vehicles had nestled among the foliage so that they were out of sight. Alex Sector and Hondo MacLean were ready for the inevitable battle with their sworn enemies.

Back in the clearing, André had more or less finished.

The others started to bicker at once.

'I'm next!' announced Dagger.

'No, *I* am,' insisted Vanessa.

'What about me?' urged Rax.

'Tell them, Mayhem!' shouted Dagger.

'Stop pestering me!' snarled the VENOM leader. 'You're like a flea on a dog.'

'But you said *my* statue was next.'

Vanessa looked at her colleagues with utter disdain. 'I'm next. Ladies before . . . ah, whatever . . .'

She did not feel able to say "before gentlemen"!

'We should do it in alphabetical order!' suggested Dagger.

'That makes me second!' complained Rax.

'And me *third*!' howled Vanessa.

'Hey!' yelled Dagger, pointing at his leader. 'How come *you* were first. "D" for Dagger is before "M" for Mayhem!'

'Not in *my* alphabet!' retorted the other. 'Dagger!'

'Yeah?'

'You're a stupid twit!'

'Does that mean I go next?'

'NO!'

The argument was interrupted by the sound of a jet aircraft. They looked up to see Thunder Hawk zooming across the sky. Hanging from its underside was the large wooden crate.

Miles Mayhem was annoyed at the sight of the aircraft.

'Those stupid MASK fools are still hanging around.'

66

'Yeah,' agreed Vanessa with a snigger. 'They're like ugly wallpaper. Wonder what the crate's for?'

'I always thought their vehicles were a bunch of crates!'

Mayhem gave a sinister laugh at his joke and the others joined in. André watched them from the top of the scaffolding. Like the VENOM agents, he could not see what MASK could do to rescue him.

The enemy seemed to hold all the cards.

Inside Thunder Hawk, however, Matt took a different view.

He and Bruce Sato gazed down on the scene below.

'This looks like a good place to open a restaurant.'

'Perfect, Matt.'

'Shall we serve dinner?'

'Make that dessert.'

'Why?'

'One "Pandy Candy" coming up.'

Bruce worked a lever on the dashboard.

The clamps released the wooden crate and it fell heavily through the air as Thunder Hawk flew on. When it hit the ground with a deafening thud, the crate split open to reveal hundreds of pounds of bamboo shoots and leaves.

The pandas responded almost immediately.

Several of them threw aside their parsnips and stood up on their hind legs to sniff the air. Other bears followed suit. Almost all of them were soon trying to catch a scent in their nostrils.

Mayhem and his colleagues looked on in confusion.

'What's happening?' said Rax.

'They don't like the parsnips any more,' noted Vanessa.

'Why are they sniffing like that?' wondered Dagger.

'I smell something fishy going on here!' decided Mayhem. 'But it ain't fish!'

A few bears started to run off in the direction that they had been sniffing. Others went after them. They began to bleat loudly as they scampered along. All the bears joined in the stampede and headed straight for the MASK agents who scattered in disarray.

'Heeeeeelp!'

'Go away, you crazy bears!'

'Yiiiiii!'

'STOP!!!!'

They huddled in a circle to avoid being trampled.

'MASK has done something to take the bears away,' said Mayhem.

'That will spoil our whole plan,' added Vanessa.

'We've got to get 'em back,' ordered the other. 'Fast!'

The VENOM team ran off to its vehicles.

Miles Mayhem climbed into Switchblade and converted to helicopter mode before taking to the sky. Vanessa Warfield jumped into Manta which remained in vehicle mode as she drove off. Cliff Dagger roared away in Jackhammer while Sly Rax brought up the rear on Piranha, the motorcycle and sidecar.

VENOM was determined to put up a real fight.

André watched from the scaffolding in total bewilderment.

'I wish someone would tell me what's going on!'

He would find out very soon.

The panda stampede had now slowed to a halt. They found the bamboo that had spilled out of the wooden crate and fell on it hungrily. They were soon enjoying their favourite delicacy and cooing happily between bites. It was much better than eating parsnips.

Thunder Hawk swooped down so that Matt and Bruce could get a close view of what was happening. They smiled with satisfaction.

'Operation "Panda Power" is in motion,' said Bruce.

'I knew it would work.'

'A panda is like an army. It marches on its stomach.'

'I bet VENOM got a shock.'

'You'll be able to ask Mayhem himself, Matt.'

'What?'

'Here he comes!'

Matt saw Switchblade descending out of the sky at them.

'It's show time, Bruce!' he noted. 'Masks on!'

Their masks automatically slid into place to cover their faces. Matt wore Spectrum, while Bruce put on Lifter once more.

Miles Mayhem was in his Viper mask.

He fired a stinger rocket that ripped past Thunder Hawk.

'That one's a warning!' he shouted. 'The next one's gonna give you a flat-top!'

Thunder Hawk fired back then rolled out of the way of the next rocket. The two aircraft began to fire at will and the air was filled with the sound of the fierce battle.

André was terrified by it all. With the sound of gunfire echoing in his ears, he scrambled down from the scaffolding as fast as he could and ran to find some shelter.

His teeth were now chattering like castanets.

'Hope I never see a piece of sculpture again!' he said, ruefully. 'I'm taking up finger painting!'

As the aerial conflict raged overhead, the statue of the VENOM leader stood in the middle of the clearing. Thanks to André's skill, it bore a hideous resemblance to its model.

Miles Mayhem's impassive stone face looked on.

The two sides were about to commence battle at ground level as well. Rhino and Firecracker were racing along at speed when Jackhammer and Piranha started to move in on them.

Seated in Firecracker, Hondo spotted them coming and spoke to Alex over the intercom. Since Bruce was still up in Thunder Hawk, Alex was driving the bulky Rhino alone.

'Looks like the animals got out of the zoo,' said Hondo.

'I'm ready for 'em!'

'Be careful. These animals *bite*!'

'Not if you take their teeth out.'

Piranha closed in on Rhino and Sly Rax grinned.

'This oughta warm you up a bit!' he sneered.

He released a blast of rapid laser fire from his front loaders. Rhino quickly converted its front grill into a battering ram to deflect the beams. As the lasers hit the ram, they splashed into star shapes and dissolved harmlessly.

'Didn't feel a thing!' said Alex with a chuckle.

It was Cliff Dagger's turn to join in the attack.

'Try this for size!' he grunted.

Jackhammer's reciprocating cannons fired continuous rounds of lasers directly at Firecracker. The MASK machine veered off to one side and screeched to a halt.

Hondo MacLean pressed a sequence of buttons.

'You need cooling down,' he said. 'Like this.'

Firecracker shot its freeze rays through its rear cannon. They met the laser fire from Jackhammer head-on. The laser fire-rods froze in mid-air then fell to the ground in glass-like pieces. Hondo started his vehicle up again and chased Jackhammer. The VENOM machine suddenly spun around and steered right at Firecracker.

A collision seemed unavoidable.

'I'll knock you to pieces!' threatened Dagger.

Hondo MacLean was ready for him with another weapon.

'Okay, VENOM. I want you to keep your eyes on mine.'

Firecracker's front headlights began to whirl with a multi-coloured strobe. Jackhammer was caught up in the hypno-headlights. Dagger's head began to sway from side to side.

'What's happening?' he said. 'I'm getting drowsy.'

'Go to sleep!' advised Hondo. 'Shut your eyes.'

'I'm being . . . hypno . . . tised . . .'

The collision was avoided at the last moment.

Jackhammer swerved off the course and went into a mad spin. It whirled into Mayhem's statue with such force that the stone began to tilt over. Dagger climbed out of his machine in a daze and staggered away from it. He was only just in time.

The statue collapsed on Jackhammer and flattened it.

Andre's handiwork was smashed to pieces.

Looking down from Switchblade, Miles Mayhem saw himself in fragments all over the clearing. His anger swelled.

'Dagger, you idiot! You ruined my image!'

Yet another VENOM dream had been shattered.

On a country road nearby, Scott Trakker was riding on T-Bob who was in motorscooter mode. The boy was holding the baby panda in his arms. All around them was the noise of gunfire.

'Can't you go any faster, T-Bob?' urged Scott.

'Sure. But not with you *and* him.'

'What do you mean?'

'Why don't you get off and walk?'

'Because we don't want to get caught up in the battle.'

'Neither do I!'

The baby panda made a noise to indicate fear.

'Neither does he!' translated Scott.

'I'm hurrying as much as I can,' said T-Bob.

'We're not gonna make it,' added the boy.

Laser fire seemed to be closer than ever now.

They were hemmed in and could be hit at any moment.

All of them began to tremble slightly.

SEVEN

Alex Sector found himself a target once more for VENOM attack. Piranha came straight at him and this time it was supported by Manta, which had its grill open and its grinding wheels turning noisily. Both vehicles fired off lasers at the MASK machine.

Vanessa Warfield was driving Manta with a vengeance.

'Rax!' she said into her microphone.

'Yeah?' came the grunted reply.

'You hit him. I'll tear him to pieces.'

'It'll be a pleasure!'

'Come here, Rhino!' she hissed. 'I want to blow your horn!'

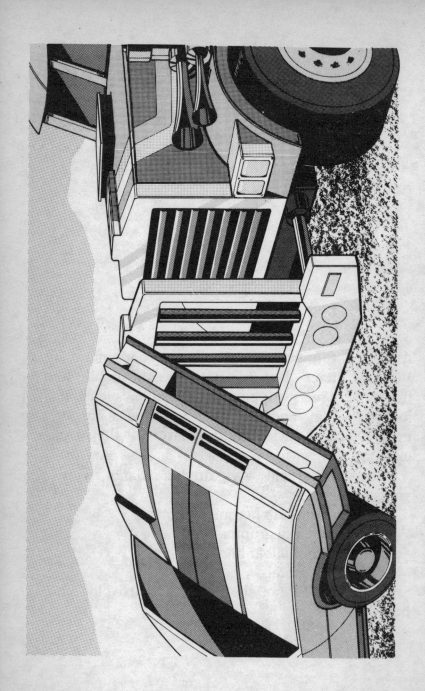

Alex saw them coming and knew how to deal with them.

'I'm gonna shake matters up for you a bit, VENOM.'

His battering ram extended a few feet in front of the vehicle. He flicked a switch and the ram went up and down, pounding the earth with such ferocious power that it caused shock waves to travel along the ground. The vibrations hit both Manta and Piranha.

'Stop!' yelled Vanessa.

'I'm bouncing all over the place!' howled Rax.

The shock waves intensified and their vehicles started to go out of control. Vanessa fought in vain to hold on to her steering wheel. Manta was being thrown about violently.

Suddenly, its wheels vibrated off. The doors fell to the ground and the engine popped out from under the hood. The entire vehicle was breaking up.

Vanessa scrambled out, shivering with fear.

'I'm getting outta here! We're on shaky ground!'

She started to run away over the shaking ground.

Alex chuckled and contacted Hondo on his intercom.

'Say, Hondo!'

'I hear you, Alex.'

'Bet you didn't know Warfield was religious.'

'Never!'

'Take a look at her now.'

'I see what you mean,' agreed Hondo, laughing.

'She's a Quaker!'

The aerial battle was continuing with unabated fury. Miles Mayhem was keeping Thunder Hawk under intense bombardment from Switchblade. Matt Trakker, however, was equal to everything that was thrown at him. He manoeuvred his aircraft with his usual skill and dodged most of the shells and lasers that were fired at him. Bruce Sato took care of the rest.

'Here comes another,' warned Matt.

'One good shot deserves another,' replied Bruce.

Mayhem's rocket was exploded before it reached them.

'This is like a ball game, Bruce.'

'Mayhem pitches and we hit the home runs.'

'Stand buy for his next one!'

Another rocket was blown to pieces well in time.

Miles Mayhem was getting progressively more annoyed.

'I'll get you!' he vowed.

'You and whose army?' taunted Matt.

'VENOM's army. The most powerful in the world.'

He fired everything he possibly could but Thunder Hawk again dodged some of it and shot down the rest. The MASK machine seemed to be impregnable.

The same could not be said of Piranha.

As the rockets exploded in the air, they showered down on the hapless Sly Rax who was still trying to attack Rhino. Lumps of hot metal fell out of the sky directly above him.

'Talk about a reign of terror!' he moaned. 'I'm gonna high-tail it outta here!'

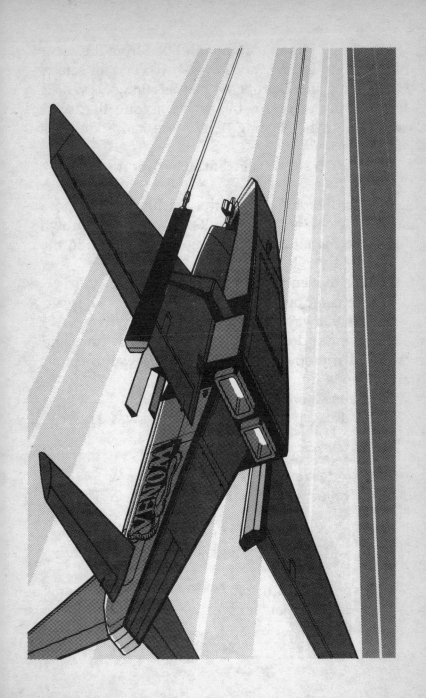

He swung Piranha around and fled from the scene of the action but he was going far too fast for safety. Not looking ahead properly, he was taking his vehicle towards the pieces of the wooden crate that were scattered in the clearing. One piece had a long nail sticking up.

Piranha's front wheel went right over it.

BANG!!!!

The tyre exploded and the machine went into a series of elaborate somersaults. Sly Rax was thrown high into the air before coming down to land in the middle of the pile of bamboos.

Pandas moved in and licked him all over.

Sly Rax came out of his daze and saw where he was.

'Hey! Get away! I'm not a stick of candy!'

The pandas decided he was a special delicacy and crowded around him even closer. He flew into a panic and jumped up.

'Leave me alone! I'm not your lunch.'

A few dozen pandas thought that he was. He raced off.

'Aaaaa!'

The pandas ran after him in a solid pack.

Matt Trakker watched it all gleefully from Thunder Hawk.

'Something tells me he doesn't like bears.'

'Pity!' added Bruce. 'They obviously *love* him.'

Sly Rax sprinted madly on. His Stiletto mask had come off now and he had no weapon to use against the

pursuing pandas. Except his two legs. He lengthened his stride to keep ahead of the bears.

Miles Mayhem gazed down from his cockpit.

'Oh no!' he moaned.

His wonderful schemes lay in ruins.

Rax, Dagger and Vanessa were all in retreat and the statue of the VENOM leader had been smashed to bits. It was an omen.

Mayhem had little sympathy for his colleagues.

'Those morons! I can never count on them when I need them!'

'Heeeeeelp!' shouted Dagger.

'Down here!' cried Vanessa.

'Rescue us, Mayhem!' howled Rax.

Switchblade came right down towards the clearing with a rope ladder dangling from it. Vanessa and Dagger dived for it and caught hold of the rope. They climbed a little way up it then Switchblade took off. Rax was left down on the ground.

The pandas had almost caught him. Desperation set in.

'MAYHEM!!!!' he shrieked.

'Okay, okay.'

'WAIT!!!!'

'I'm coming back.'

'Let me get in on this trapeze act!'

Switchblade dipped down again so that the rope ladder flailed about in front of the VENOM agent. With the bears breathing down his neck, he launched himself at the ladder and grabbed hold of the bottom rung. As Switchblade rose up, however, one of the pandas got a grip on the seat of Rax's trousers.

RIP!!!!

A large piece of material was torn away.

'Ohhhh!!!!'

Sly Rax went bright red with embarrassment.

His colleagues teased him. Vanessa gave a wolf whistle.

'You're a man after my own heart!' she said.

'Hey, Rax,' mocked Dagger. 'You left a bear behind!'

'Shut up, you two!' warned Rax.

Switchblade was making its escape across the sky.

'VENOM is getting away,' noted Bruce Sato.

'Let them go,' decided Matt Trakker. 'We've got to take care of the pandas.'

Mayhem's voice boomed out once more.

'I'll find another island, MASK!' he boasted. 'You'll see. I'll be back!'

'We'll be waiting for you,' promised Matt.

Thunder Hawk banked, then headed down to Easter Island.

Scott, T-Bob, Alex and Hondo were waiting as the MASK machine made a perfect landing in the clearing. André came running over to greet his friend. The sculptor was delighted that the fighting was over.

Matt and Bruce got out of Thunder Hawk.

'Time to give that little fella back,' noted Matt, pointing at T-Bob. 'Come here.'

'*Me*!' said the robot in alarm.

'No, T-Bob. Baby.'

Matt took the little panda from the incubator and set it down on the ground. Its parents immediately ran over from the group of pandas munching bamboos nearby. There was a touching reunion.

'Congratulations, everybody!' announced Matt. 'Great work. We saved the pandas, rescued André and preserved these stone statues from further disfigurement. The Chinese government is going to be very pleased with MASK.'

'Looks like we have another assignment,' observed Bruce.

'What?'

'To rescue T-Bob,' explained Scott. 'Look, Dad.'

The parents of the baby panda were delighted to see their offspring again. Loping over to T-Bob, the father bear began to lick him gratefully and make slurping sounds. It lifted him up.

'Hey!' said T-Bob. 'What does he think he is – a papa robot?'

'That's just a little ol' bear hug,' replied Scott. 'I think you've been adopted, T-Bob.'

Everyone laughed at this except the robot himself.

'Oh no – I don't even have fur!'

The panda licked him with obvious relish.

'Scott, you've got to help me!' pleaded T-Bob.

The boy took out a piece of bamboo from his pocket and offered it to the panda. It seemed to understand that a bargain was being struck.

'Want some panda candy? I'll do you a swap.'

T-Bob was promptly dropped on the floor as the animal grabbed the bamboo instead. He munched it joyfully. The robot picked itself up off the ground. Scott had the last word.

'MASK may have licked VENOM,' he said. 'But Panda Power certainly licked you, T-Bob.'

Easter Island echoed with their happy laughter.

If you have enjoyed Panda Power, you might like
to read some other MASK titles from Knight Books

MASK 2 – PERIL UNDER PARIS

Why does VENOM – THE VICIOUS EVIL NETWORK
OF MAYHEM, have a hideout in Paris? Are they
plotting to steal the paintings from the Louvre, or
have they a far more terrible, even deadly,
purpose?

When MASK discovers that VENOM holds a map
of Paris' underground sewage system with some
very strange locations marked onto it, they soon
realise that a terrible danger threatens the city.

The MASK mission: to save Paris from VENOM's
appalling evil. Matt Trakker, Buddie Hawkes, Scott
and T-Bob are the MASK agents dedicated to
foiling the plot before it is too late.

KNIGHT BOOKS

MASK 1 – THE DEATHSTONE
A meteor, which in the right hands can be the key
to a life-saving technique for mankind, but which
in the wrong hands can prove a lethal enemy, falls
to earth in the rocky desert. When VENOM come
by it, and plan to sell pieces of it off as powerful
weapons, MASK has a vital mission before it.

MASK 3 – VENICE MENACE
VENOM leader Miles Mayhem's evil scheme to
dominate the world, has brought Venice – the city
of canals – to a mysterious halt. But MASK is close
at hand.

MASK 4 – BOOK OF POWER
The revered Book of Power, holder of mystical and
ancient secrets, is sought by VENOM's leader,
Miles Mayhem, whose wicked intention is to turn
its power to his own ends.

KNIGHT BOOKS

Five stunning MASK adventures from Knight Books